Barbie™

5 BOOKS IN 1!

Barbie
PRINCESS Charm SCHOOL

Barbie
A fairy secret

Barbie
A Fashion Fairytale

Fairytale Favorites

Barbie in
A Mermaid Tale

Barbie and the
Three Musketeers

Random House 🏠 New York

Contents

Blair Willows was excited—she had won the lottery to attend Princess Charm School, the most prestigious school in Gardania! At Princess Charm School, girls were trained to become princesses and Lady Royals, trusted princess advisors. Blair knew her life as a hardworking waitress was about to change forever.

The headmistress, Madame Privet, handed Blair a school uniform and assigned her a sprite named Grace.

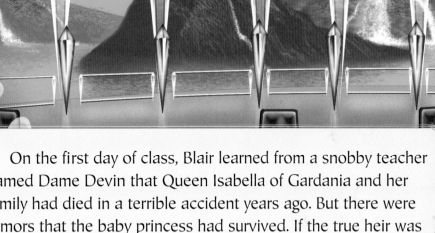

On the first day of class, Blair learned from a snobby teacher named Dame Devin that Queen Isabella of Gardania and her family had died in a terrible accident years ago. But there were rumors that the baby princess had survived. If the true heir was not found, Dame Devin's daughter, Delancy, was next in line for the throne.

Dame Devin didn't like Blair—or any other students—stealing the spotlight from her daughter.

Delancy and her mother did their best to get rid of Blair, but Blair worked hard for many weeks. Soon she outshone Delancy in all their classes.

Dame Devin was furious. She secretly had Blair's and her roommates Isla's and Hadley's uniforms destroyed. According to the Princess Charm School rules, students who didn't attend classes in uniform were expelled!

When the girls discovered their uniforms ripped to shreds, they didn't know what to do. "Coronation Day is only two days away and we'll be expelled!" Hadley exclaimed.

"I have an idea," Blair declared confidently.

Soon Blair and her friends were sewing the tattered pieces into stylish outfits.

Minutes later, the three friends raced to their etiquette class.

"Those aren't school-issued uniforms!" Dame Devin cried.

"They are made from our original uniforms," Blair said. "We just used some hard work to unlock our princess potential."

Dame Devin fumed. She wanted to get Blair thrown out of Princess Charm School—fast.

The next day, Blair, Hadley, and Isla discovered a portrait of
Queen Isabella as a young woman. The queen looked just like Blair!
    "You must be her daughter, Princess Sophia!" Hadley cried.
    "You're the rightful heir to the throne, not Delancy," said Isla.
    From her hiding place in the shadows, Delancy also saw the
resemblance and was shocked.

Blair, Hadley, and Isla returned to their room to find Dame Devin waiting for them. The teacher had secretly hidden her jewels in the girls' room and accused the girls of stealing.

"Lock them up!" Dame Devin cried to the guards.

Luckily, Delancy released the three friends. She knew Blair was the true heir to the throne and wanted to help her. Delancy gave the girls a map of the palace and told them where Gardania's Magical Crown could be found. The crown would reveal the truth: it only glowed when it was worn by the true heir of Gardania!

Blair, Hadley, and Isla quickly followed the map to a secret vault and found Gardania's Magical Crown.

Suddenly, Dame Devin appeared and snatched the crown from its pedestal. "You'll never be more than a poor lottery girl!" she cried to Blair.

Dame Devin slammed the door and reset the password on the keypad. The girls were locked in the vault!

Isla had perfect pitch and remembered the tune of the password Dame Devin had typed into the keypad. Blair hooked her phone to the back of the keypad, and Isla typed the tune into the phone.

The vault opened, and the friends tumbled out the door to freedom!

Blair and her friends raced through the palace and burst into the palace ballroom.

"I am Princess Sophia, daughter of Queen Isabella!" Blair declared.

Dame Devin tried to grab Gardania's Magical Crown, but Grace and the other fairy assistants were too quick. They whisked the crown away and placed it on Blair's head.

The crown magically glowed brighter and brighter, and Blair's outfit transformed into a beautiful royal gown.

"It is Princess Sophia!" the crowd gasped.

"No!" cried Dame Devin as she was taken away.

Blair was thrilled to be crowned Princess of Gardania. "I promise to always work hard and live up to my princess potential," she said.

To thank her for all her help, Blair asked Delancy to be her Lady Royal.

"I would be honored . . . Your Highness," Delancy said with a smile.

The friends hugged and went into the palace to celebrate. They knew that in every girl was a princess with dreams that sparkled brightly.

It was the premiere of Barbie's latest movie. Everyone was excited and happy—except for Raquelle, Barbie's costar. Angry that Barbie was getting all the attention, Raquelle had a wicked idea. She stepped on Barbie's gown—and ripped it!

Carrie and Taylor, Barbie's stylists, sprang into action. They fixed Barbie's gown by magic—fairy magic, that is. No one knew that Carrie and Taylor were fairies from a beautiful fairy world called Gloss Angeles.

The ruler of Gloss Angeles was Princess Graciella. Everyone adored the princess—except for Crystal, her royal attendant. Crystal was in love with Graciella's boyfriend, Zane, and wanted to steal him away. So Crystal gave Graciella a magic potion that made her forget about Zane and fall in love with Barbie's boyfriend, Ken.

The next day, Princess Graciella and her attendants traveled to the human world. They quickly found Ken and dragged him off into the sky.

"We're going to get married!" Graciella declared.

Barbie and Raquelle couldn't believe their eyes.
"It's time you learned the Fairy Secret," Taylor said.
"Carrie and I are fairies." Taylor told the two friends that
Princess Graciella was also a fairy. If Ken married her,
he would have to stay in Gloss Angeles forever.
"We've got to save him!" cried Barbie.

Carrie and Taylor brought Barbie and Raquelle to Lilianna Roxelle. "She's the oldest and wisest fairy living in the human world," explained Carrie.

Lilianna believed that the princess was under a love spell and gave Barbie a magical mist to break it. Then Lilianna showed them a secret passage to the fairy world. . . .

"It's incredible!" Barbie exclaimed. "I can't believe it's real."
Barbie and Raquelle bought beautiful clip-on wings. They
tried flying, but a huge gust of wind knocked them down.
Luckily, they were caught by some winged ponies.

The girls rushed into the royal palace and tried to rescue Ken. Graciella was furious! "Freeze!" the princess cried, and she trapped Barbie and Raquelle in a fairy cage. Then the princess used her magic to make Ken propose to her. Soon they would be married—and Ken would be trapped in the fairy world!

Barbie and Raquelle tried to escape from the fairy cage, but the bars were too strong.

"I'm sorry I've been so mean to you," Raquelle said to Barbie. "Can you forgive me? Do you think we can be friends?"

"We *are* friends," Barbie said as she gave Raquelle a big hug.

Their forgiveness was so powerful that suddenly, the fairy cage disappeared and the girls' clip-on wings transformed into beautiful *real* wings.

Using their new wings, the two friends flew as fast as they could to stop the wedding. Princess Graciella threw sparkling balls of light at them, but Barbie and Raquelle were too fast. Barbie flew overhead and sprinkled the magical mist on Graciella—and the spell was broken!

The princess immediately remembered that she loved Zane, not Ken.

Zane proposed to Princess Graciella, and she happily said yes. The couple decided to get married on the spot—with Barbie, Raquelle, Carrie, and Taylor as their bridesmaids.

Princess Graciella realized that Crystal had given her the love potion, so she gave her attendant a fitting punishment: Crystal had to clean up after the royal wedding reception!

"Thank you for breaking the spell," Graciella told the three friends. "You are always welcome to come back to Gloss Angeles."

"Wait until we tell people about this place!" said Raquelle.

But Princess Graciella cast a spell on Barbie, Ken, and Raquelle. They would believe that their time in the fairy world was all a dream—and Gloss Angeles would remain a fairy secret.

Back in the human world, Carrie and Taylor said goodbye to Barbie, Raquelle, and Ken. They had to return to Gloss Angeles.

"I had the strangest dream about being in a fairy world last night," Raquelle told Barbie. "And I woke up feeling like we're friends."

"I had the same dream," Barbie replied with a smile. "But I *know* we are friends—good friends."

"Look!" Barbie exclaimed to her pet poodle, Sequin. "Paris!" Barbie was so excited. She was flying to France to visit her aunt Millicent at her famous fashion house.

When Barbie arrived at Millicent's, she was greeted with a warm hug. But Aunt Millicent had some bad news. "I'm closing my fashion house and moving to the country."

Aunt Millicent's assistant, Alice, told Barbie why Millicent's was closing. A mean designer named Jacqueline and her assistant, Delphine, had stolen all Millicent's fashion ideas and sold them as their own. Now no one wanted Millicent's designs.

Barbie was sad. "When I was younger, I used to think Millicent's was a magical place," she confided to Alice.

"I think it still is," said Alice. "Legend has it that magical creatures could be summoned from inside this antique wardrobe to help fashion designers."

The two girls quickly placed a dress that Alice had designed inside the wardrobe and closed the doors. Suddenly, the wardrobe was filled with sparkling lights. Then three Flairies flew out.

"We are Glimmer, Shimmer, and Shyne," said the Flairies. "We give flair to fashions we love!"

Barbie and Alice looked in the wardrobe. Alice's dress glittered and sparkled. It was fabulous!

Barbie had an idea. If she and Alice held a fashion show and sold lots of dresses, they could save Millicent's!

Barbie and Alice cut and sewed beautiful new outfits all night. And the Flairies used their magical powers to make each new design glimmer, shimmer, and shine.

Meanwhile, Jacqueline was spying on Millicent's. When she spotted the Flairies, she cried, "I have to make them mine!"

Jacqueline and Delphine kidnapped the Flairies and demanded that they glitterize their fashions. But Shyne said, "We don't love these dresses. If we use our magic on them, we don't know what will happen."

Jacqueline didn't believe Shyne's warning. She was going to have her own fashion show—and on the same day as Millicent's!

That night, as everyone slept, Sequin awoke to bright sparkling lights coming from Jacqueline's. It was the Flairies! They were using their magic to light up the store window and get the pets' attention.

Sequin and her new animal friends quickly rescued Glimmer, Shimmer, and Shyne from the mean designer's fashion house.

The next day at Jacqueline's fashion show, her models were walking down the runway when suddenly, their dresses turned into garbage! The Flairies' magic had worn off!

"This can't be happening!" cried Jacqueline.

The crowd was horrified and quickly left.

At Millicent's, Barbie and Alice were relieved that the Flairies had returned safe and sound. But Alice was nervous. What if the audience didn't like their outfits?

"We put our heart and soul into these designs," Barbie said. "Now let's rock this party!"

Barbie walked down the runway wearing the creations from Millicent's fashion house. After each spectacular design, the crowd burst into applause. And as Barbie modeled the final outfit, the Flairies added a little extra glimmer, shimmer, and shine. Everyone cheered!

Millicent's fashion show was a hit!

After the show, many orders were placed for the beautiful designs. The fashion house was saved!

"Magic happens when you believe in yourself," said Alice.

"Especially with a little help from Glimmer, Shimmer, and Shyne!" Barbie cried.

Merliah Summers smiled as she rode the waves. Ever since she was a little girl, Merliah had been able to swim like a fish. Now she was one of the best surfers in Malibu.

As Merliah surfed, she thought everything was perfect—
until she noticed her hair. It was *turning bright pink!*

Shocked and embarrassed, Merliah wiped out and dove below the waves. To her amazement, she found that she could *breathe underwater!*

"Merliah?" someone said. A sparkly pink dolphin w talking to her! "My name is Zuma. I am a friend of your mother, Calissa. She is the mermaid queen of Oceana—but she needs your help."

Merliah couldn't believe that her mother was a magical mermaid—and that she was half mermaid herself! Merliah learned that when she was a baby, her mother's wicked sister, Eris, had taken over Oceana. The fortune-telling Destinies had foretold that Merliah would one day defeat Eris. So to protect her baby daughter, Calissa had sent Merliah to live with her human grandfather in Malibu.

Merliah agreed to help and followed Zuma to the underwater kingdom of Oceana.

She didn't want anyone to know that the young surfer was in Oceana—especially not Eris.

Zuma quickly brought Merliah to the boutique run by her friends Xylie and Kayla.

"Tail makeover!" Xylie and Kayla exclaimed.

At the palace, Eris snuck down to the secret dungeon where Calissa was locked away. The evil mermaid had learned that Merliah was in Oceana.

"Tell me where she is," Eris snarled at Calissa.

But Calissa refused to answer, to protect Merliah.

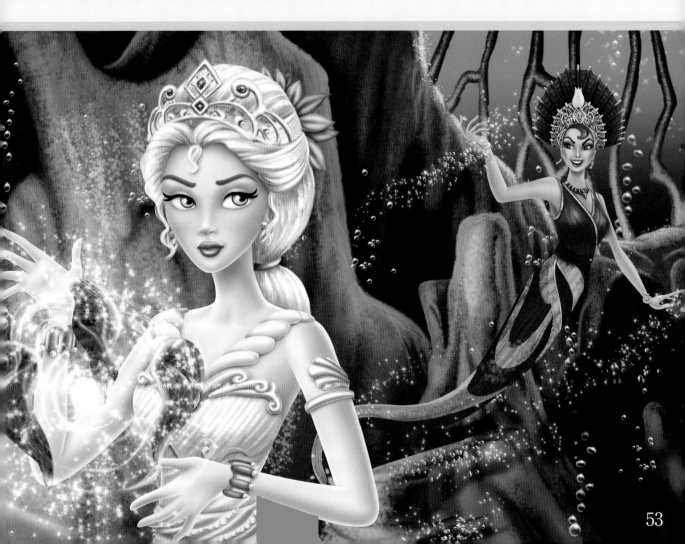

Meanwhile, the Destinies had told Merliah how to stop
Eris. She needed to complete three important tasks.
    The first task was to find the Celestial Comb, hidden in
the Yafos Caves. No mermaid could climb the steep rock wall
to reach the comb. But Merliah had legs, and she scaled the
wall quickly. "I've got it!" she cried triumphantly.

The second task was to impress a dreamfish so that it would grant her a wish. Zuma knew exactly where the dreamfish could be found: in the Adenato Current. The powerful swirling water was impossible to swim in—but Merliah could surf it! The dreamfish were amazed.

"Call when you need me, and I will come," promised one young dreamfish.

55

The third task was the hardest. Merliah needed the necklace that Eris always wore around her neck. Merliah knew that Eris would appear at her daily festival, so she came up with a plan. Merliah, Xylie, and Kayla started singing to distract Eris.

"You're the queen of the waves!" sang the friends.

As Eris watched the show delightedly, Merliah snuck up behind her—and snatched the necklace!

"Stop her!" Eris cried.

The evil mermaid's manta sharks swam after Merliah and ripped off her fake tail!

"You!" Eris cried, realizing that Merliah was Calissa's daughter. Eris quickly captured the young surfer in a powerful whirlpool.

Merliah called for the dreamfish. He appeared and offered to return her to her normal life in Malibu. Merliah was tempted. But her mother and Oceana needed her, so she decided to stay and help.

Suddenly, Merliah's legs magically transformed into a sparkly *real* mermaid tail. Merliah couldn't believe it!

"I am Merliah, half-mermaid princess of Oceana," she cried proudly, and leapt out of the whirlpool. "And it is my duty to protect my subjects."

"Get her!" Eris ordered her guards.

"You don't need to listen to her," Merliah said. "I am the rightful heir to the throne. I have the Celestial Comb!"

Enraged, Eris tried to push Merliah back into the whirlpool. But Merliah quickly swam out of the way. The wicked mermaid was sucked into the powerful swirling water and transported to the deepest, darkest trench in the ocean.

The crowd cheered. Eris was gone forever!

Calissa was overjoyed to see her daughter. She wanted Merliah to stay in Oceana. Merliah was happy, too—but she missed her human life in Malibu. Calissa hugged Merliah and placed a magical necklace around her neck. Whenever she wished on the necklace, Merliah could transform from human to mermaid—and back again. "Then you can move easily between the human world and the underwater world," Calissa said.

Merliah was thrilled that she would have a home in both worlds!

In a small village in France, there lived a beautiful girl named Corinne who loved to fence. Corinne dreamed of one day becoming a Musketeer and protecting the royal family in the city of Paris.

When she arrived in Paris, Corinne met with Monsieur Treville, the head of the Musketeers.

"I want to be a Musketeer," Corinne said. "Please give me a chance."

Unfortunately, she was told that she did not have enough experience and training. Corinne was heartbroken!

With no other choice, Corinne gratefully accepted the royal
housekeeper's offer to become a maid in the castle. Everyone was busy
preparing for a special masquerade ball for Prince Louis. He would
become king in a few days.

But the prince's royal advisor, Philippe, had other ideas.
Philippe believed that he should be king, so he came up with
a plan to get rid of Louis.

As Prince Louis walked through the castle's great hall, one of Philippe's men sent the chandelier crashing down—narrowly missing the prince!

Then the ceiling started to collapse! Corinne and three other maids quickly sprang into action. They smashed, cracked, shattered, and broke all the falling pieces. Thanks to them, no one was hurt.

The three maids were named Renée, Viveca, and Aramina.

"Where did you learn to move like that?" asked Renée.

"Ever since I was a little girl, I've dreamed of being a Musketeer," Corinne said.

"So have we!" said the other maids.

Every day, the four friends secretly practiced. They wanted to prove to everyone that they could be Musketeers.

The day before the masquerade ball, Corinne noticed men sneaking swords into the castle. She tried to warn the guards that the prince's life was in danger, but they didn't believe her. To make matters worse, Philippe ordered Corinne and her friends to leave the castle—and never return!

The girls would not give up, so they came up with a plan to save Prince Louis.

"All for one and one for all!" Corinne, Viveca, Renée, and Aramina cried together.

The night of the masquerade ball, Corinne, Viveca, Renée, and Aramina disguised themselves in gorgeous gowns. No one recognized them as they entered the castle.

When Prince Louis saw Corinne, he could not take his eyes off her. "May I have this dance?" he asked.

As they twirled across the floor, Corinne noticed that Philippe was holding a *real* sword.

Suddenly, Philippe and his men surrounded Louis.
But the girls were ready!
"Prepare for battle!" Corinne shouted.
The four friends quickly used their swords, ribbons, fans, and
bow and arrow to stop Philippe's men.

But Philippe wasn't through yet—he was determined to
get rid of Louis and become king himself. So he kidnapped
the prince and took him to the castle's rooftop. Luckily,
Corinne was right behind them!

Corinne and Philippe drew their swords.

Clang! Clang! Clang! Corinne soon knocked Philippe's sword
from his hand.

"Match over!" she cried.

Corinne, Renée, Aramina, and Viveca had proved that they were brave, so the prince declared them Musketeers.

"All for one and one for all!" the four friends cried.